HarperFestival is an imprint of HarperCollins Publishers.

Transformers: Hunt for the Decepticons: Prime Target
HASBRO and its logo, TRANSFORMERS, the logo and all related characters
are trademarks of Hasbro and are used with permission. © 2011 Hasbro. All Rights Reserved.
Manufactured in China.
No part of this book may be used or reproduced in any manner whatsoever without written
permission except in the case of brief quotations embodied in critical articles and reviews.
For information address HarperCollins Children's Books,
a division of HarperCollins Publishers, 10 East 53rd Street, New York, NY 10022.
www.harpercollinschildrens.com

Library of Congress catalog card number: 2010922246
ISBN 978-0-06-199180-6
Book design by John Sazaklis
11 12 13 14 15 SCP 10 9 8 7 6 5 4 3 2 1
❖
First Edition

TRANS FORMERS
PRIME TARGET

HUNT for the DECEPTICONS
TRANSFORMERS.COM

Adapted by Susan Korman

Illustrated by MADA Design, Inc.

HARPER FESTIVAL
An Imprint of HarperCollinsPublishers

"I'll tell him!"
"No, *I'll* tell him!"
Optimus Prime finally interrupted the bickering twins.
"Please, somebody just tell me! Is Sam safe?"

"Since Bumblebee is away on a mission, we've been watching him, like you asked," said Mudflap.
"And there's no sign of Decepticons?" Optimus asked.

The twins hesitated. "Well . . ."
"What is it?" asked Optimus.
"Sam is working on a supermagnet project in the science lab," said Skids. "There's a new research assistant—"

"And we think he's a Decepticon spy," Mudflap finished. "Then keep your eyes on him!" Optimus ordered. "And don't let Sam out of your sight either!"

Meanwhile Megatron, the Decepticons' leader, was plotting new ways to defeat the Autobots. "First I must destroy Optimus Prime," Megatron declared.

Then an idea came to Megatron. Optimus had a weak spot—it was the boy, Sam Witwicky! Megatron could use the boy to lure Optimus!

The new lab assistant *was* a Decepticon spy. Soon he was carrying out a special order from Megatron: Hack into Sam's computer and send a phony message to Optimus Prime!

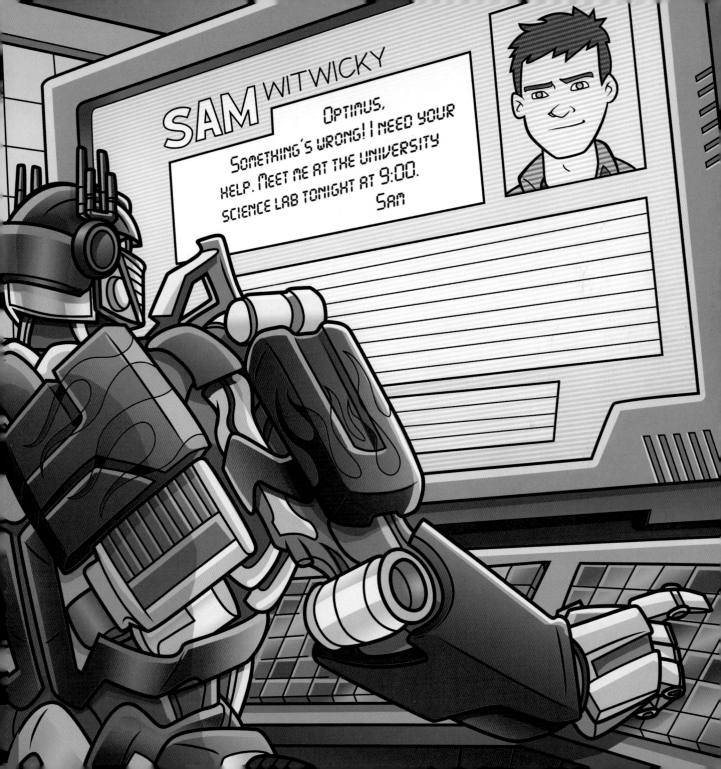

Optimus sped to the university to help Sam.

The science lab was pitch-black. When a light flickered inside,
Optimus caught sight of something. Megatron!

"Sam!" yelled Optimus. He revved his engine and crashed through the wall.

But as Optimus drove right into the building, he crossed the supermagnet's field. It pulled him in!

Optimus furiously tried to free himself. But the supermagnet's force was too powerful.

Suddenly, Megatron flipped a switch, releasing Optimus. "Now I will destroy you!" the Decepticon bellowed.

Optimus faced his enemy, ready for battle. But when he tried to change modes, he couldn't! The magnetic field had caused a malfunction!

Megatron raised his massive claws and pounded Optimus again and again. Optimus shot into reverse, trying to get away. He spun, and then . . . *boom!*

Optimus slammed into a wall—and went completely still.

"At last!" Megatron cried. "I've stopped the mighty Optimus Prime!"

As Megatron stepped closer, Optimus suddenly blasted forward. He smashed into the Decepticon at full speed and sent him hurtling toward the supermagnet.

"Optimus!" someone shouted. It was Sam. "The Decepticons sent you a phony message!"

Sam ran into the lab and turned on the magnet. The machine whirred to life. Now Megatron was pinned there helplessly!

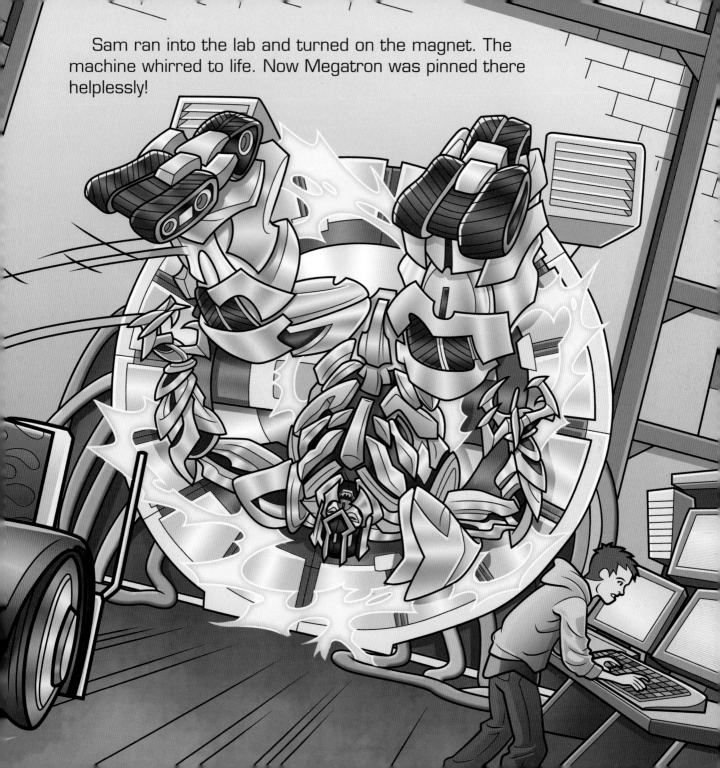

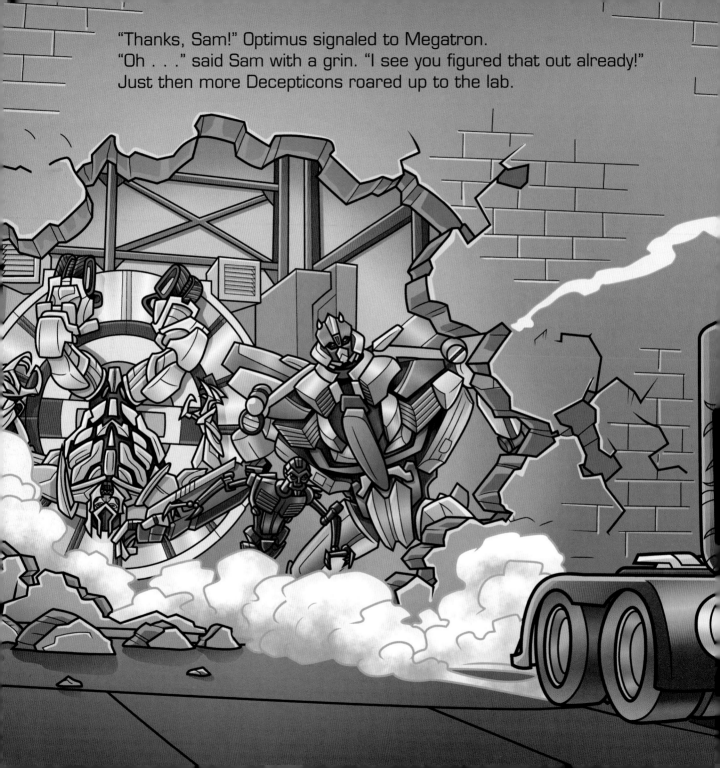

"Thanks, Sam!" Optimus signaled to Megatron.
"Oh . . ." said Sam with a grin. "I see you figured that out already!"
Just then more Decepticons roared up to the lab.

"Come on!" Optimus said. He wanted to get Sam out of there.
"Where are we going?" Sam asked.
"To find Ratchet," said Optimus. "I have to get my power back!"

"So can we stop spying on Sam now?" Skids asked Optimus.
"You messed up Megatron's plot," Mudflap reminded him.
"Sorry, twins." Optimus shook his head. "Our battle against
the Decepticons is far from over."